BERNARD WISEMAN

Little New Kangaroo

Pictures by ROBERT LOPSHIRE

Ready-to-Read

MACMILLAN PUBLISHING CO., INC.
New York
COLLIER MACMILLAN PUBLISHERS
London

Macmillan Publishing Co., Inc., 866 Third Avenue, New York, N.Y. 10022
Collier-Macmillan Canada Ltd., Toronto, Ontario
Library of Congress catalog card number: 72-92444
Printed in the United States of America

10 9 8 7 6 5 4 3 2 1

The pictures were drawn in pen and ink line with halftone overlays
for brown and green. The text is set in Century Schoolbook.

Library of Congress Cataloging in Publication Data
Wiseman, Bernard.   Little new kangaroo.   (A Ready-to-read book)
[1. Kangaroos—Stories.   2. Stories in rhyme]   I. Lopshire, Robert,
illus.   II. Title.   PZ8.3.W75Li   [E]   72-92444
ISBN 0-02-793220-6

Little New Kangaroo

Little new

kangaroo . . .

Mama hops —
out he pops!

He falls down.
He yells, "Ouch!
I fell out
of the pouch."

Mama says,
"Hold on tight.
Then you will
be all right."

Little new

kangaroo . . .

Now he knows

what to do.

He says, "Look —
look who's there!
A new
koala bear!
Hello, friend.
Come inside.
Sit with me.
Take a ride!"

Little new
kangaroo
tells the bear
what to do.
"Hold on tight!
Hold on tight!
Hold on with
all your might!"

Mama hops.
She hops high.
The bear yells,
"You can fly!"

They see a
bandicoot
eating a
piece of fruit.
Little new
kangaroo
yells, "Come on —
you come, too!
Come inside.
Have a seat,
and give us
fruit to eat."

He gives them
each a bite.
They tell him,
"Hold on tight!"
Mama says,
"Please sit still
while I hop
up that hill."

Mama hops.
Up they go!
But her hops
now are low.

Mama says,
"Puff . . . puff . . . puff.
No more friends!
Three's enough."

Then they see
a wombat.
He is round.
He is fat.
He yells, "Fruit!
I want some.
I love fruit—
let me come!"

Mama yells,
"Please — no more!
I cannot
carry four!"

Little new
kangaroo
cries, "Mama,
take him, too!
You are big.
You are strong.
You can take
him along!"

Mama gives
a big sigh.
She says, "Well . . .
I will try."

Mama hops.
Mama sweats.
Oh, how tired
mama gets!

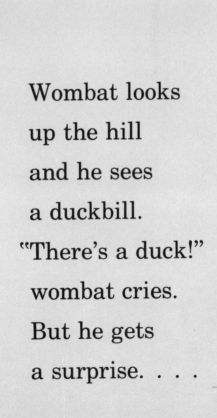

Wombat looks
up the hill
and he sees
a duckbill.
"There's a duck!"
wombat cries.
But he gets
a surprise. . . .

It has hair
on its back
and it does
not say quack!

Bandicoot
starts to laugh.
He says, "Look —
half and half!"

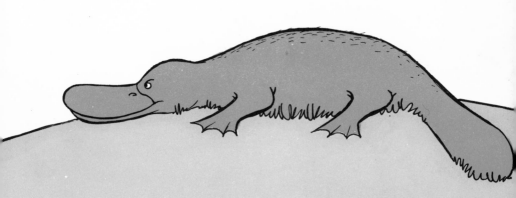

Mama yells,
"Shame! Shame! Shame!
Platypus
is his name!"

Platypus
looks so sad
they all feel
very bad.
Little new
kangaroo
says, "Hello!
How are you?"
Mama says,
"Platypus,
climb in here —
come with us."

Mama hops
for a while.
Platypus
starts to smile.
Mama says,
"Puff . . . I think
I would like
a cool drink."

They all drink.

Glup! Glup! Glup!

Mama says,

"Hurry up!

It is late.

We must go.

Bedtime is

soon, you know."

They all cry,
"Let us stay!
We all want
time to play."

They play games.
They have fun
till there is
no more sun.
No more sun,
no more light . . .
it is dark.
It is night.
Mama cries,
"Climb in fast!
Let us see
who is last."

Wombat's last!
They all joke,
"Wombat is
a slowpoke!"

They all yawn.

Mama hops. . . .

At each home

mama stops.

Parents say,

"Be polite.

Wave your paw!

Say, good night!"

Little new

kangaroo . . .

Soon he is
at home, too.
He has made
four new friends.
Now he sleeps.
His day ends.